A Note to Parents

Welcome to REAL KIDS READERS, a series of phonics-based books for children who are beginning to read. In the classroom, educators use phonics to teach children how to sound out unfamiliar words, providing a firm foundation for reading skills. At home, you can use REAL KIDS READERS to reinforce and build on that foundation, because the books follow the same basic phonic guidelines that children learn in school.

Of course the best way to help your child become a good reader is to make the experience fun—and REAL KIDS READERS do that, too. With their realistic story lines and lively characters, the books engage children's imaginations. With their clean design and sparkling photographs, they provide picture clues that help new readers decipher the text. The combination is sure to entertain young children and make them truly want to read.

REAL KIDS READERS have been developed at three distinct levels to make it easy for children to read at their own pace.

- LEVEL 1 is for children who are just beginning to read.
- LEVEL 2 is for children who can read with help.
- LEVEL 3 is for children who can read on their own.

A controlled vocabulary provides the framework at each level. Repetition, rhyme, and humor help increase word skills. Because children can understand the words and follow the stories, they quickly develop confidence. They go back to each book again and again, increasing their proficiency and sense of accomplishment, until they're ready to move on to the next level. The result is a rich and rewarding experience that will help them develop a lifelong love of reading.

To Alex and Michael—
this book is for you.
—M. B.

Special thanks to Hanna Andersson, Portland, OR, for providing
clothing; to Converse for providing sneakers; to Raynor Suter
Hardware, Mattituck, NY, for providing cleaning supplies;
and to Julianna Carlson for her drawing.

Produced by DWAI / Seventeenth Street Productions, Inc.
Reading Specialist: Virginia Grant Clammer

Library of Congress Cataloging-in-Publication Data
Bernstein, Margery
   That cat! / Margery Bernstein ; photographs by Dorothy Handelman.
      p.   cm. — (Real kids readers. Level 2)
   Summary: A cat sleeps soundly despite all the activities going on around her.
   ISBN 0-7613-2019-9 (lib. bdg.). — ISBN 0-7613-2044-X (pbk.)
   [1. Cats—Fiction. 2. Sleep—Fiction. 3. Stories in rhyme.] I. Handelman,
Dorothy, ill. II. Title. III. Series.
PZ8.3.B45854Tf 1998
[E]—dc21   98-10045
                                                           CIP
                                                           AC

                    pbk: 10 9 8 7 6 5 4 3 2 1
                    lib: 10 9 8 7 6 5 4 3 2 1

That Cat!

By Margery Bernstein
Photographs by Dorothy Handelman

M

The Millbrook Press

Brookfield, Connecticut

How do you do? My name is Pat.
This is the story of Boots, my cat.
I know you've heard of a cat in a hat.
I call *my* story "The Cat on the Mat."

The Cat On The Mat

By Pat

5

Into a room
there came a cat.
Near the door
she saw a mat.

The room was warm.
The room was still.
"I will sleep here,"
she said. "I will."

Boots went to sleep.
Then in came Spot.
He barked and barked.
He barked a lot!

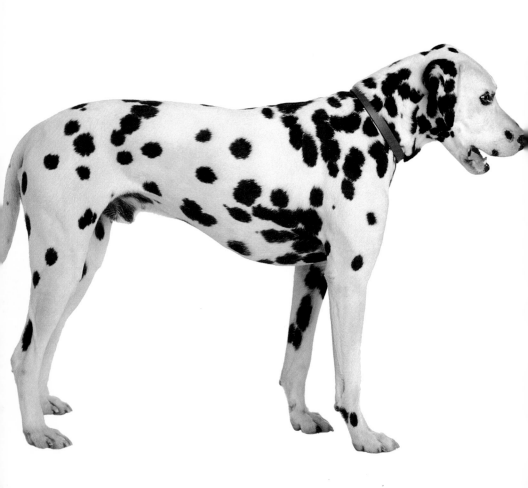

That dog was mad.
"Get off!" he said.
"That is *my* mat.
That is *my* bed."

Boots did not hiss.
She did not leap.
That cat slept on.
Her sleep was deep.

The door went BANG and Jan came in.
She talked and joked with Jack, her twin.

They left. Again, the door went BANG.
They made a lot of noise, that gang!

But Boots slept on.
She was not ill.
She just turned once
and then lay still.

Jan looked and looked
around the hall.
"Hey, Jack," she called.
"Where is my ball?"
"Up here," yelled Jack.
He dropped the ball.
It bounced downstairs
into the hall.
The sound was heard
all over town.
(Boots did not blink
or even frown.)

17

18

Next Hal came in.
He saw the cat.
"My train goes here,"
he said. "So scat!"

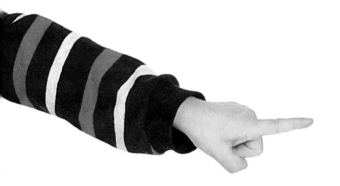

He put his toy train
on the track.
It started up
and went CLACK CLACK.

20

The train went by that cat's soft bed.
It went right by her little head!
She did not jump or run away.
She did not move from where she lay.

Next Dad came in
and mopped the floor.
He left the pail
close to the door.
Then Jack ran by
and bumped the pail.
The water spilled
on Boots's tail!

The cat slept on.
She did not stir.
The mat was wet.
So was her fur.

Her tail was wet,
yet there she lay.
Would she move now?
Not now! No way!

Then Dad said, "Pat,
please get some fish.
It's for the cat.
We'll fill her dish."
When I began
to open the can,
the cat dashed in.
Yes, in she ran.

That cat was there,
right at my feet—
the fastest cat
you'd ever meet.
She purred and purred.
She would not sit.
Was she tired now?
No, not a bit.

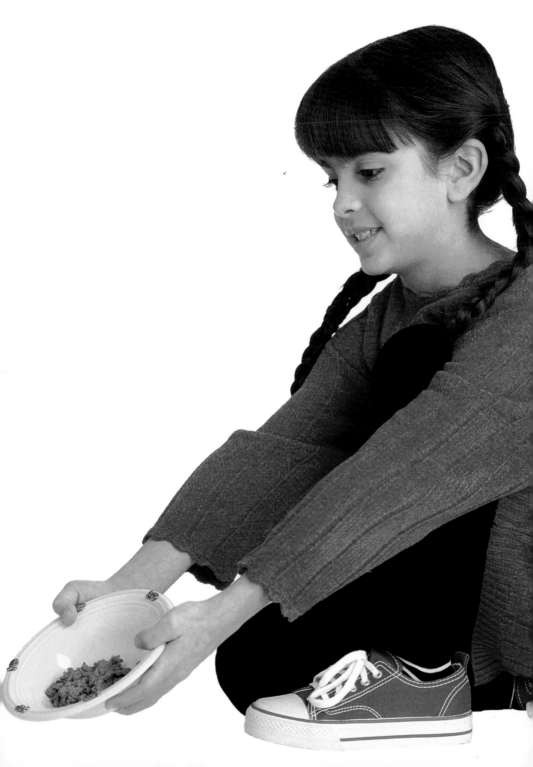

What woke up Boots
I cannot tell.
Was it a sound?
Was it a smell?
What made her jump
right off the mat?
What do *you* think
woke up that cat?

Phonic Guidelines

Use the following guidelines to help your child read the words in *That Cat!*

Short Vowels
When two consonants surround a vowel, the sound of the vowel is usually short. This means you pronounce *a* as in apple, *e* as in egg, *i* as in igloo, *o* as in octopus, and *u* as in umbrella. Short-vowel words in this story include: *bed, bit, but, can, cat, Dad, did, dog, get, Hal, hat, his, Jan, lot, mad, mat, not, Pat, put, ran, run, sit, wet, yes.*

Short-Vowel Words with Consonant Blends
When two or more different consonants are side by side, they usually blend to make a combined sound. In this story, short-vowel words with consonant blends include: *bang, blink, bumped, clack, jump, just, left, next, scat, slept, soft, Spot, track, twin, went.*

Double Consonants
When two identical consonants appear side by side, one of them is silent. In this story, double-consonants appear in the short-vowel words *fill, hiss, ill, smell, spilled, still, tell, will, yelled,* and words in the *all* family: *all, ball, call, hall.*

R-Controlled Vowels
When a vowel is followed by the letter *r*, its sound is changed by the *r*. In this story, words with r-controlled vowels include: *barked, fur, purred, started, stir, turned, warm.*

Long Vowel and Silent E
If a word has a vowel and ends with an *e*, usually the vowel is long and the *e* is silent. Long vowels are pronounced the same way as their alphabet names. In this story, words with a long vowel and silent e include: *came, close, made, name, tale, tired, woke.*

Double Vowels
When two vowels are side by side, usually the first vowel is long and the second vowel is silent. Double-vowel words in this story include: *deep, feet, lay, leap, meet, pail, please, sleep, tail, train, way.*

Diphthongs
Sometimes when two vowels (or a vowel and a consonant) are side by side, they combine to make a diphthong—a sound that is different from long or short vowel sounds. Diphthongs are: *au/aw, ew, oi/oy, ou/ow.* In this story, words with diphthongs include: *bounced, down, frown, how, noise, now, saw, sound, town, toy.*

Consonant Digraphs
Sometimes when two different consonants are side by side, they make a digraph that represents a single new sound. Consonant digraphs are: *ch, sh, th, wh.* In this story, words with digraphs include: *dashed, dish, fish, that, then, there, they, think, this, where, which.*

Silent Consonants
Sometimes when two different consonants appear side by side, one of them is silent. In this story, words with silent consonants include: *Jack, know.*

Sight Words
Sight words are those words that a reader must learn to recognize immediately—by sight—instead of by sounding them out. They occur with high frequency in easy texts. Sight words not included in the above categories are: *a, and, about, again, around, away, by, do, even, ever, from, goes, he, her, here, I, in, into, is, it, little, looked, move, my, near, no, of, off, open, on, once, over, said, she, so, some, the, to, up, was, would, you.*